CATBOY AND THE NEW EVIL

GRACE E. TUTTLE

Balboa Press books may be ordered through booksellers or by contacting:

Balboa Press
A Division of Hay House
1663 Liberty Drive
Bloomington, IN 47403
www.balboapress.com
1 (877) 407-4847

ISBN: 978-1-9822-3741-7 (sc)
ISBN: 978-1-9822-3742-4 (e)

Print information available on the last page.

Balboa Press rev. date: 10/21/2019

CATBOY AND THE NEW EVIL

Bing! The bell rang for school and the teacher Ms. Morgan began to call roll.

"Michael."

"Hi, here."

"This is the first time you have been on time in a week," said Ms. Morgan. "He's not the only one. A lot of you guys still think it summer. Half fall asleep in class. Enough! Now wake up. This is English class."

It was the second week of school, September 1st. There was still Summer weather and most of us wished we could be at the community pool or out on our bikes. She was right: we needed to shape up. This class was mostly all Juniors at Brokland High School.

She continued to speak to the class: “In this class I will push you to your limits and I expect you to be on your best behavior now that you’ve been warned. For your first big assignment, I want you come up with a creative story. It’s going to be five pages long and I want it done by this Friday.”

Yes, this was my Junior year. I was looking forward to all the cool things that come with being a Junior but also knew it meant I’d have to study hard for my parents. They wanted us do well.

“The story can be true or not true. It could be about dragons, magic or something you did over the summer. It could also be your favorite hero. Now I have pencils and paper for you and Amber here is going to pass them out.” Said Ms. Morgan

This year is going to be fun. I’m going to join the year book club and do my best. I hope there are no big bad guys that try to end the fun for me. I’m going to spend time with my best friend James. He’s been in my life a long time.

Michael began to do his assignment and write about what he did with his family, Alex and Tony, his brother and sister, and his mom and dad. They went to Las Vegas where he enjoyed playing video games and site seeing.

He also was Cat Boy, a local hero, but he didn't want give that away. It was too risky. What if a bad guy knew that his name at school was Michael? He took out a lot of bad guys doing the summer. Of course there were lots of bad guys in big bad Las Vegas. That was his best part of his summer.

BOOM!

Cat Boy felt powerless but there nothing he could do without showing everyone his big secret. Right now he was just plain Michael. They were in school and everyone was yelling a screaming for help because they just heard a bomb go off close by. What should everyone do? The kids ran around in panic. Michael just wondered how he could help to do something other than wait for instructions from his English teacher .

“Everyone calm down,“ said Michael.

“Yes, now I want you all to line up in an orderly fashion,” said the English teacher.

They headed outside to the school playground and waited for the principle, Hun Yang, to come and give the next instructions. He came out quick and wasted no one’s time.

“Hello everyone! Please be quiet while I give you the following announcement: once the police arrived they found out the bomb was just a cherry bomb it didn’t do that much damage. But it was found in our school,” said the principle.

"It was in the school parking lot and it destroyed my car. I'm very upset and whoever did this will be expelled immediately!" said the principle, Hun Yang.

"They will ask some questions and then you can all go home. We will have a whole day tomorrow!"

Everyone was in deep shock about what happened. Mr. Yang is usually nice so why target him and as a principle he didn't have a lot of money.

The police came by and said that anyone can say a word. There was a pack of them lining out the gate to the school where we usually go home and come in at. They had their guns, flash lights, and dogs with them. And through the crowd I saw a friendly face: it was my friend in the force, Halloo. I think the dogs were confused by my cat smell because they kept smelling me a lot and barking in playful way.

They started asking everyone the same questions: did we notice anything strange or unusual happening? Were any friends of ours acting up? But Halloo took me to where they found the bomb and asked for my help .

He asked, "Do you smell anything unusual or weird or see anything with those cat eyes of yours?"

"Yes, I smell perfume and honey." said Cat Boy.

"Ok, what else?" said Halloo.

"I see a woman's shoe by the car ."

They pulled out a shoe that was small and in parts. It looked like they had lost it in a hurry. The shoe read a size four. It was definitely a woman's shoe.

The drill lasted half the day. As it went by people began seeing that it wasn't just a drill. It was a bomb that went off near the school, about one block away. Cat Boy was a regular student and he didn't want to cut school to go after this criminal. During lunch he sat by his best friend named James wondering who could have done such a thing like blow up a house like that.

Michael and James were eating their school lunch together. For lunch they had tacos and a salad.

The bomb was found in the basement of someone's home. Luckily no one was home and not much was missing. The air was filled with smoke so the playground was off limits. Julio gave everyone a mask to wear.

Michael was glad he only had two periods left for the day. His plan was to interview the person who lived there right after school. He heard from Julio that the house was on 1200 Main St.

He and Julio became great friends over the summer when they often worked on cases together. One person had tried to rob a caddy store. It was both funny and sad—what can you get from robbing something like that where there's very little money? They only got a year in jail time, which is not much.

It became foggy and the fog mixed with the smoke that filled the air. It was hard to see your hand in front of your face. His mind was going over the clues that he had been told: a woman's shoe, a car, and the weird smell of honey.

Bing! Rang the bell for end of lunch.

It was still the beginning of the school year and Michael was thinking of the nice letter he got from his Grandfather Wilson. It was nice to hear from him. Even though Thanksgiving was weeks away, knowing he would be there for the holiday made him happy.

It's now night. I have the scent of the woman's shoe and now I'm trying to find her. I'm working with my dad and a permanent partner. I'm wearing an invisible earpiece so that he can talk to me whenever I get into somewhere that I think the criminal is because they smell like the suspect that I'm after or look like the person that I'm after.

My cat eyes help because I can see far into the night. That's why I do crime fighting at night. I'm right on the trail of the woman's scent. It's coming from a pink and white house that smells like roses. I go in the house through an open window.

Thump, tap, rattle squeak! The floor makes a noise of shoes walking his direction. The light goes on in the living room.

"Aww Cat Boy, what are you doing here?"

"Ms. Ginger! The teacher!?" He was in shock that the scent that he was following led him to a house where someone he knew lived.

"Wait, do I know you?" Ms. Ginger said to him, "How do you know who I am and what I do?"

Cat Boy replied, ""You're a teacher to a friend of mine, James...I mean...ummm, I know you because I go to the school where you teach. I'm a student you know. I can't give my name but I go to your school. Ms. Ginger, where were you today? James, my friend didn't see you in school."

"You break in to my house. I'm the one who should be asking the questions!" As she shone the light in Cat Boy's eyes.

"Ok, just calm down. I'm on a tail of a criminal. I'm here because I asked the victim, whose name is Mr. Pow, if he heard or saw anything out of the ordinary today. He said he saw a strange woman leaving in a hurry. He'd never seen her before and he gave me a shoe that was left behind on the scene. The smell from the shoe led me to your home. Did you go by the school to a house on 1243 Maple? It's a blue and green house where Mr. Pow lives."

"Because I've read about who you are and what you do I will not call the police. To answer your question, yes I was there at nine in the morning. He's my doctor and friend that I go to see for mental health. He has a private office there. I have known Mr. Pow for 15 years, since I was in school. I have known him since I was a little girl" said Ms. Ginger. "I told him about someone that can possibly give him home to stay in until they fix his house. Yes, when I knew just who was hit I went to see if he was ok. Ok, maybe there will be another clue to that will lead you to the right person. Now if you will kindly leave, I would like to get some rest and go to bed."

"Thanks for your help Ms. Ginger," said Cat Boy.

That was odd. I didn't want to give away who I was under the mask and hero suit. I leapt out of the window and onto the roof, thinking to myself, *she goes to the school and is a teacher so she should be the person I'm after.*

After getting on the roof I saw something in the middle of 43 High St. There I found a clue: a map of the city and it had targeted places where to strike next. At a house uptown by the park there will be a big hit in the day, again at 9:45. A boom is to go off in the morning at Piedmont Ave.

I need to find the guy or woman tonight or maybe I'll have to cut school? I can't cut school though; I have to rejoin the group. I'll have to work with my dad and tell him that I found this new important clue.

Cat Boy left for home. He was about to give up but he knew there was still time. He went home to think things over. His folks would be missing him. His dad knew he was a super hero at night so he agreed to let him use his cat power at night to continue that act of hero work. It was get very late and he thought it was best for him to return home.

I called him for a lift home and he came fast in his cool FBI car. The question I had was what was he or she looking for and why the bombs looked like they were planned at random locations?

“Good work son, it’s 10:50. You should have been in bed if you were normal person but we let you stay up so you can help fight for justice for the town.”

“Thanks dad! I enjoy having you help full time now instead of before when I was doing this alone.”

“Look, the good thing about my job is that it looks like I can pull some strings to get to help in day time to make this an FBI investigation. That way you don’t have to miss any school.”

“Thanks dad! I love you and we make the best team.”

"Son your dinner is in the refrigerator and your brother and sister are worried about you a little so you can relax. I told them I'll help with your fighting skills so you'll be ready and with me helping you with balance, I got this. I promise to be the best team captain you'll ever have."

"Yes seeing that you're my only team captain I'll ever have to have."

They got home safe and sound. They ate dinner together with just the small dining room light on so they wouldn't wake anyone. The father worked on Cat Boy's report on his new job. Cat Boy had to report everything he did to his dad, and his dad to his boss.

The next day his dad went in to look where the bomb had gone off on the map clue his son had given him. Alex and Michael gave him a big hug at the breakfast table. They didn't want anything to happen to their bother.

Alex: "Good morning! Did you get your bad guy? How was your night?"

Michael: "Good morning! It was interesting but I didn't get him or her yet."

Alex: "WOW! I'm in the eighth grade now so next year I'll be with my big bother! Is that cool or what?"

Michael: "Cool I'll have to tell all the boys to stay away from you and protect you. I'll show you where your locker is and do all the things our older brother did for me."

"Yes, high school is fun—prom and other things like being on the baseball team and finding out which after school club you can join. This my last year and I'll have to start looking for colleges for next year soon. Best to stay ahead! I want to be an artist or do something in music," said the oldest brother.

"It time to go school, you guys. Get in the car." The mom honked the horn to get their attention.

"I'm also starting to look for a job so I can get my own car. I'm going to need it for college," said the oldest son .

The mom drove on and continued to listen to the kids as they talked about their future.

“Mom, I’m going to be a teacher for little kids or a cop or a doctor. I want to give back to the next generation,” he said .

“I want to be a vet at the zoo when I grow up and go to a UC when I grow graduate from high school.”

When they got to school James Grant gave them a big hug then started talking about the day before: “What’s up? Man, it was crazy yesterday every one running around like scared cats.”

“I was on the baseball field but couldn’t get to you since we have different first period classes this year,” said James

“Yes, I know. I was trying my best not to panic but today we go back to the regular program,” Tony said.

They went to their classes and waved good bye.

“Good morning, class! Yesterday we didn’t get to much so today we have some catching up to do. We’ll start the class with a book reading. It’s such a good book we’re reading: ‘Where the Red Vine Grows.’”

Cat Boy shared every night with his dad, working with him. In the day his dad would interview people in the neighborhood and he would tell his son everything he found out. While cat boy was Michael during the day he had to go school.

When he saw Ms. Ginger the next day he was afraid that she knew he was Cat Boy and she would tell people. Now it was the third day into the mystery and the bombs kept coming. There was a small clue who was a women she would make small mustache t people would say it was say they smelled her perfume and the have a voice recording from her she left as clue. The voice recording said that she wanted to rule the world as a queen or she would keep destroying something very important to us if she didn’t get what she wanted—our complete loyalty to her.

He was going to meet his father tonight with more information. His dad’s boss was able to identify the person who was doing this act of great evil. With a voice identifying machine. And once he heard the voice he knew very well who it was himself because he had work closely with her once before.

“Wow what a tall building.” said Tony

“England is so big and so wide and different,” said Alex.

“Yes it is. It’s not like home. This hotel is great. I’ll wait with our daughter. That woman makes all of us look bad. She is wicked,” said the mother.

“Yes” said Cat Boy, Dad, and Dad’s boss all at once.

The other team was waiting downstairs.

“Common, we may only have a few minutes till her plan falls into place and we don’t when or where she might strike next!” said Ginger.

They went into the fast FBI Car because they are official car’s for chasing and they were able to go through all the lights. In the middle of England they were waiting with ever thing in place.

“Men and women, there are 120 of them to take down and only 6 of us. We are outnumbered by great deal. They have weapons of mass destruction.”

"Now Cat Boy, remember your training! Now is not the time to panic," said Ginger. "There is a very large bomb and if someone doesn't get over there to dismantle it soon, the town will be in great danger and a lot of lives will be gone."

"You are all going to die today! Cat Boy this will be your last time to try to stop any one!"

"You are going to pay for this and you'll be the one going down tonight!" said Cat Boy.

"Every one act then."

Bang, bang, running, pushing. The bad guys let out everything they had. They had guns, lasers, and everything went off at once and they were good at fighting. Cat Boy leaped into action remembering someone had to get had to get the bomb.

"You fight them off. I'll try to go for the bomb and dismantle it before it's too late."

In the sky was a getaway helicopter. It also had an automatic gun with someone shooting from the sky.

"I'll help take out the pilot," said Ginger.

"We'll fight off the others, leaving you to take out the pilot," said his father.

"Me as well. Don't worry about us, just go with her."

I run left, right—dodging bullets as I go, starting to climb a building near the helicopter.

"I need a boost from here!" said Cat Boy.

The helicopter pilot seemed to notice them because he moved twelve more feet in the air.

Ginger opened her hands for the boost and then Cat Boy looked up. He knew if he looked down he'd be afraid and wouldn't make the leap. He had never leapt this far up in his life. Everyone was counting on him.

He bounce jumped into the air. His eyes were staring right at the pilot. She was shocked to see that he was going to make it.

"Cat Boy, oh no!"

The woman pilot tried to jump down with a parachute but Cat Boy stopped her. Now they only had ten minutes until the bomb went off and it would kill other people.

"Wait, I can help you! I know the code you need to stop the bomb. Please, if I help will you let me go?" said the woman.

"You still have to go to jail but if you help us we might help you get off quicker if you stop that bomb for us"

"No! We were so close to getting the world's power!"

The other agents were still fighting hard just to stay alive. It was 119 to five down below.

"Looks like this one wants to be on our side."

Cat Boy helped the woman to get to the bomb and then Danna attacked him while her best friend was putting in the code next. It was xgh98740jk. Letters and numbers. Who would have thought that would be the code to stop the bomb?

The fight was over.

The bad guys boss surrendered. They all went down and to jail .

With one exception we did help Alice that was the women turned against Danna .

"Wow, I'm glad that's over."

"Me too, son. Me too," said dad.

"Rower" went Cat Boy because he was very happy that it was all over.

"Now let's go back to the hotel. Thanks boss for paying for us to stay the next two weeks after this. We need a vacation and he's going to be an exchange student so they all will be here for a while." said Cat Boy's father.

Good night every one lest all go back to the hotel for well earn rest .

They went to the hotel and went upstairs. They went to the dinner hall and the grown ups drank wine or other drinks with a nice lamb dinner. They were rejoicing over a great victory.

THE END.

Printed in the United States
By Bookmasters